Royal Gambit

by Hermann Gressieker

Translated and Adapted
by George White

A SAMUEL FRENCH ACTING EDITION

SAMUEL FRENCH

FOUNDED 1830

New York Hollywood London Toronto

SAMUELFRENCH.COM

ROYAL GAMBIT was presented for the first time in English by David Ellis on March 4, 1959, at the Sullivan Street Playhouse, New York City, with the following cast:

KING HENRY VIII.....................*Russell Gold*
KATARINA OF ARAGON...................*M'el Dowd*
ANNE BOLEYN ....*Tani Seitz*
JANE SEYMOUR.....................*Dolores Rashid*
ANNA OF CLEVES.................*Alice Drummond*
KATHRYN HOWARD.................*Elizabeth Perry*
KATE PARR ....*Grace Chapman*

Directed by Philip Lawrence
Setting designed by Glenn Hill
Lighting by Nicola Cernovich
Costumes by Michael De Marco

TIME—*Sixteenth century to the present day.*
PLACE—*England.*

NOTES

In this play Henry VIII represents one type of modern man The aspects of the modern age develop through the erotic and moral tragi-comedy of his life. The historical affairs with the six wives transcend history. But it is not suggested that Henry stalks through history or through the centuries; merely that he and his wives are aware of the further developments and the logical conclusions of what he began. Thus the sweep into the future occurs effortless in dialogue only. But if these passages are not sharply indicated, if their beginnings are not carefully presented, then they might tend to confuse and become extremely difficult to enact

Throughout the play Henry must remain constant in costume and make-up, while the dresses of the women should suggest, in a discreet styling, the passage of time from the renaissance to the present.

The scenery should be as simple as possible. Props are not to be used, and it is essential in this play that no other characters (pages, etc.) are ever brought on stage.

Royal Gambit

ACT ONE

*FOOTLIGHTS only. The SIX WOMEN are kneeling next
to each other, facing the audience They are veiled,
but as each one's name is mentioned, she removes
her veil Behind them, dimly visible, is a large
crucifix*

HENRY'S VOICE. (*Sincerely, evenly*) I, Henry Tudor,
take you, Katarina of Aragon, to be my only wife and
promise, that I will love you and keep you unto death —
I, Henry Tudor, King of England, take you, Anne
Boleyn, to be my only wife and promise, that I will love
you and keep you unto death — I, Henry Tudor, take
you, Jane Seymour, to be my wife,—take you, Anna of
Cleves, to be my wife,—take you, Kathryn Howard, to
be my wife,—take you, Kate Parr, to be my wife and
promise, that I will love you and keep you unto death
So help me God!

(*Each* WOMAN *rises before her speech*)

KATARINA OF ARAGON (*Severe, but without affecta-
tion*) So help him God!—The truth is, I alone was his
wife unto death, and I still am in our existence beyond
time
ANNE BOLEYN The truth is, he gave up one world to
win a new one with me, and he loved me—unto my
death
JANE SEYMOUR I gave him what he cherished more
than love; I presented him with the male heir
ANNA OF CLEVES (*With grim humor*) I was the one
who knew him as no other woman did, and we could have
had much fun, had it only pleased him—to have me.

5

KATHRYN HOWARD I found the aging man weak in his manly vigor, and I brought joy into his life again, so that he loved me murderously!

KATE PARR I am the one he did keep unto death, although I insisted that he face up to what he was, and where it would lead, the age that he began

ANNE BOLEYN The age that he began, he and the others—

KATE PARR —greater men than he—

ANNE BOLEYN —was the age which we, in our spirited revolt, called, "The Modern Times"

KATARINA OF ARAGON The first age of the world which was not to be God's, but man's It became a great age of man and of his brain The old order—it so happened—collapsed simultaneously with my marriage It went under at that moment when he, my husband, God's great apostate (*To* ANNE BOLEYN) looked upon you

(ANNA OF CLEVES, KATHRYN HOWARD, KATE PARR *exit effortlessly to the Right and Left At the same time full LIGHTS on stage Room in Westminster* JANE *and* ANNE, *as ladies in waiting, stand behind* KATARINA *A royal FANFARE*)

HENRY (*Enters pompously, in a good mood, waving a scroll and shouting*) Defender of the Faith! I am— Defender of the Faith!

KATARINA Oh, my husband! It has pleased the Holy Father to bestow upon you the apostolic title?

HENRY It has finally pleased the Pope to grant me what has been long overdue

KATARINA A wonderful reward for your struggle against heresy

HENRY The rent due for my defense of the sacraments against that miserable Luther Fortunate England, to have as king a great theologian!

KATARINA Fortunate England, if you preserve it as a strong island of our church.

HENRY. (*Concentrating on the ladies in waiting.*) How could I fail—my dearest—?

KATARINA. (*Carefully.*) I hear that three more convents have been confiscated in your name and to the advantage of your treasury.

HENRY (*Struts up and down in front of the ladies in waiting, who withdraw a little. He takes* JANE *by the chin and raises her face. Over his shoulder, to* KATARINA.) Your Jane Seymour looks pale. Could it be she, too, needs a young poet to chase her with his verses like a doe? Eh, Boleyn? Why do your eyes sparkle so? What?

ANNE. (*Maintains a stubborn silence.*)

HENRY. Well! What are you thinking?

ANNE That Your Majesty must be an excellent physician The pale Jane has turned crimson You have cured her by humiliating me.

HENRY. I humiliate you? Not me! That Tom Wyatt! Couldn't you prohibit him from calling you a doe?

ANNE. Couldn't you prohibit Luther from calling you a jackass? (KATARINA *laughs heartily.*)

HENRY. (*Stunned for a moment, then crashing, jovial laughter*) She has a quick tongue, the doe—to my taste. (*Close to* ANNE, *with compelling gaze.*) But I think the doe needs our Royal protection.

ANNE. (*Anguished*) The Queen is in audience with Your Majesty.

HENRY. (*To* KATARINA, *insignificantly.*) Indeed you are, my love But I don't intend to strain your patience much longer with my confounded theology. You may go—leave Boleyn here for a while. She needs a bit of advice

KATARINA. (*With slight irony.*) As you wish.

(HENRY *avoids her gaze. She hints a curtsey and exits with* JANE ANNE *maintains a guarded manner while* HENRY *walks around her in a big circle.*)

HENRY. (*Suddenly*) What about you and Tom Wyatt?

ANNE. What about Your Majesty and Thomas Moore? And Erasmus? And Holbein? What about you and Tom Wyatt?

HENRY. My acquaintances are gifted thinkers and artists, as I myself am. But it's not proper for a lady-in-waiting to become involved with a poet.

ANNE. I was educated at the court of Paris, and I think I know very well what is proper for a lady in our days. I fully subscribe to the teachings of humanism as they reach us from an enlightened Italy. And Your Majesty, who is truly the Augustus of the new spirit of the universe—Your Majesty shall not treat me as would an insignificant country squire who clings to the old order, (*Contemptuously*) the gothic.

HENRY. Girl, how dare you answer me? Don't you know me in my terrible majesty?—Take it as a sign of my extreme favor that I'm not punishing you. And now —(*Drags her before the crucifix.*)—tell me before His face, what about you and Tom Wyatt?

ANNE. Your Majesty is not my father confessor

HENRY What are you to him?

ANNE. It's written in his poems for all to read. He calls me the run away doe

HENRY (*To himself.*) Holy Mercy, I thank you! (*Different tone of voice, intimately.*) Come, my dear, sit down beside me (ANNE *sits down hesitantly*) You're not kind to me, Anne. You're so distant. Why? Don't I deserve better? Didn't I grant your sister Mary my affections for five long years?

ANNE I know well how to appreciate that. I love the little boy you presented her with

HENRY. And didn't I make your father my treasurer?

ANNE (*Pointedly*) A favor duly honored by those who know the circumstances

HENRY But you, Anne! Under my very eyes, you have developed more magnificently than any other woman in my kingdom (ANNE *withdraws from his advances.*) What stubborn pride! Incredible!

ANNE. I watched my sister carry on with many men at the French court. La petite Boleyn! People always

talked about her—even before you took her And I
don't intend—if Your Majesty's extreme favor is based
upon such an inclination—to follow the way of my sister.

HENRY. What can I do to make you love me?

ANNE Be good enough to leave me be, and I shall love
you as is my duty toward my King

HENRY. (*Jumps up*) King! King! What, King? I am
a man! (*Expression of self-admiration*) Look at me as
I stand before you Look! My accomplishments in the
tournaments and at wrestling are justly famous even
among the Turks. As for the pleasures I can give a
woman—ask Mary No, better not! (*Holds out his
biceps*) Here, feel this! 'Tis harder than your forehead!

ANNE. 'Tis hard as stone! And for that I should love
you?

HENRY. (*Naively*) And why not?

ANNE. Let me feel your heart, how hard that must be.

HENRY (*Distressed*) Oh, you don't understand me.
You don't understand because I keep saying the wrong
things And why do I keep saying the wrong things?
Because you make my heart beat so quickly it clouds my
brain. That's why! Now you know it!

ANNE You frighten me—

HENRY (*Crowding her*) Oh, delicious Anne Boleyn!
You will give yourself to a man of your own choice, and
to no other! You will choose one who is devoted to you,
and completely yours, now and in all eternity I am that
man!

ANNE. You—Your Majesty—so—"justly famous"—

HENRY. Oh, don't listen to my boasts! I beg you to see
me as I really am, so poor, so miserable, a man of thirty-
five, just reaching out to put my imprint on history,
but—irrevocably tied to a woman—a good woman, to be
sure, rich in grace of body and spirit, but—a Spaniard,
and thus incurably afflicted with the old order, unable to
follow me to a new, enlightened existence And, what is
worse, a woman not blessed to give me the son! This
marriage, arranged to strengthen England through an
alliance with Spain, it weakens England in England.

ANNE (*Tortured*) Your Majesty is pleased to show me only the dark aspects—

HENRY. Just as my despair seems hopeless, my gaze falls upon Anne Boleyn, and I shudder with happiness. My God has sent you to me, so that I shall not fail in my great mission. No! That I may achieve it with you at my side And thus I'm yours, Anne Boleyn.

ANNE Oh, Sire, how could that be!

HENRY Let me woo you.

ANNE No!

HENRY. Let me woo you as Jacob wooed Rachel.

ANNE You would soon tire of it.

HENRY. I shall do it, and were it indeed seven years.

ANNE (*Determined*) No, don't!

HENRY. I'm at your service

ANNE (*Clear-sighted*) I know it cannot be, not now, and not in seven years

HENRY I'm at your service

ANNE I enjoin you from it

HENRY I'm at your service.

ANNE I flee to my father's house at Hever (*Walks slowly to the Left, ascends a few steps and sits down.*)

HENRY I write to you—I beg you to return

ANNE I remain at Hever

HENRY I beseech you to return

ANNE I remain at Hever.

HENRY I threaten to turn my back on you.

ANNE I recommend it to you

HENRY I come to Hever. (*Walks to her*) I come to see your father on business, as if I were his servant, and not he mine I'm at your service—and you know it. My knees tremble I, your King, am blushing

ANNE I remember your prowess in the tournaments and laugh

HENRY I'm miserable! I crawl back into my gilded jail (*Walks back*) I write more letters I beg you for a small sign of your favor

ANNE I compose a tender letter—as to my uncle on his patron saint's day

HENRY. I devour drunkenly each tender word. I read

it once more and tear it to shreds with my teeth, and my hands are empty once again and I cry out for more.

ANNE I will not hear you.

HENRY. I'm at your service. I kneel before you. What more do you want? Do you want me to idolize you?

ANNE. By all the saints, no!

HENRY. By all the saints, Anne, tell me how I may win you at last?

ANNE (*Walks to him slowly; there, quietly but determined*) You could if you were to belong to me, were mine . .

HENRY (*Sobs with rapture, reaches for her.*)

ANNE —in all your splendor, mine alone!

HENRY (*After a pause, composed*) I knew you would demand it I could not expect less

ANNE I demand nothing, Your Majesty! I merely answered your question.

HENRY (*Aside, inflexible tone of voice.*) If any man in Catholic Christendom is justified to separate from his wife because she is barren, I am that man! But marriage is a sacrament, and as Defender of the Faith, I just can't do it

ANNE (*Walks slowly to him Simply and sincerely*) Then let us part, Henry Tudor Know that I'm beholden to you But, by your love, grant me my peace, and think of your own.

HENRY (*Broodingly*) I'm thinking of the peace of my soul The thought rakes my brain

ANNE (*Taken aback*) What do you mean?

HENRY I can't separate from my lawful wife —The question is only   (*Hesitates, then determined, controlled outburst*) The question is only, is she my lawful wife!

ANNE Our Queen?

HENRY When we were coupled, she was already a widow

ANNE Your brother's widow

HENRY The Scriptures forbid marriage with a brother's wife

ANNE The Pope has blessed it

HENRY   But not heaven

ANNE   You have a daughter

HENRY   One daughter and four miscarriages! It is obvious to me heaven frowns upon this marriage!

ANNE. You are too critical of yourself.

HENRY. I don't know —I only know— (*Buries his head in her lap.*) that I want you, woman. I must have you! . . And . . (*Looking up, suddenly enlightened.*) what is the same, I must purge my conscience of this sinful marriage.

ANNE   (*Her eyes closed, dazzled*) I love you, Henry Tudor

HENRY   Love is too frail a word for what unites us! (*He kisses her, then, very soberly and determinedly.*) I will talk with the good woman for both our souls' sake

ANNE   (*Shuddering*) Oh, my Lord, what are you about to do?

HENRY   (*Simply*) What is right.

ANNE. May heaven preserve your good intentions

HENRY   My good intentions? That's it, my good intentions! Or .   could it be possible I have something in mind that could not be well intended? No! (*Exits.*)

ANNE   (*Looks at him*) Thus you take your wife by the hand and inform her in a friendly manner that your marriage is null and void   And you expect the woman to understand! This woman who has known you since you were a boy of ten   You inform her of the dire need of your conscience Just then her gaze falls upon me (*She attempts to withstand that gaze*) Now she knows what sort of dire need it really is   . Katarina of Aragon   . her mother was the great Isabella of Spain, her nephew is the German Emperor With his support she fights for her marriage. My king, in his madness, discards the policies of Cardinal Wolsey, designed to give England supremacy in Europe He argues with his friends and advisors He throws it all over . . to bed with a girl The King of England becomes the laughing stock of Europe Spain holds him in check, for three long years. At last the Pope consents to dispatch a legate to hear Henry's lament. He arrives, and we see him surrounded by the nobles of the realm, as he convenes the tribunal.

(*LIGHTS change. A TRUMPET BLAST.*)

ANNE. They are calling the royal plaintiff! (HENRY *enters, his walk and facial expression suggesting penance*) They are calling the royal counter-plaintiff.

KATARINA. (*Enters, but maintains her ceremonial walk for only a few steps. Upon seeing* HENRY, *falls to her knees before him.* HENRY *attempts to pull her to her feet, but fails He makes a helpless, apologetic gesture to the front, where the assembly presumably meets.* KATARINA *has been speaking throughout.*) My Lord! For the sake of the love we once shared, and for the love of God, grant me justice! My Lord! Have I not always been a dutiful wife? Whom you loved, I have loved. Whom you avoided, I have avoided. All my being and all my doing is rooted in you . . . My Lord! I beseech you, listen to the true call of your conscience, and leave me my rights and my honor! But should you not grant me this small favor, then I shall suffer it and entrust my case to Him, who judges all of us Amen. (*She rises and attempts to leave. TRUMPET BLAST.*)

ANNE. Katarina of Aragon, the tribunal has not given you permission to leave.

KATARINA. No tribunal has the right to sit in judgment over my marriage . only my husband. His verdict I will accept. (*Walks with regal bearing to the Left, but once there, she calls desperately*) . . Seymour! . . Seymour!

JANE SEYMOUR (*Comes running from Left*) Milady!

KATARINA Oh, Jane, what have I done! (*They remain on stage in a dim light,* KATARINA *ponderingly,* JANE *concerned over her. TRUMPET BLAST.*)

HENRY Most reverend gentlemen, forgive her! She is a woman and—Spanish Also, it *is* true, she has always been a good and faithful companion However, you have not assembled here to concern yourselves with her conscience, but with mine, which is weighted with grave concern, as I went to considerable length to explain in the memorandum that I submitted to this high ecclesiastical court (*With naive cynicism*) In it, truthfully recorded, you will find how my first doubts arose about the sanctity of this marriage, how I continued in spite of the terrible torture it caused me, to explore these doubts until I arrived at the crushing conclusion that God was displeased Later, I found this confirmed in the tragic and premature demise of our children For that reason I find myself compelled, being deeply concerned with the future of the realm —I mean to say, most reverend gentlemen, I came to the conclusion that my God has called upon me to suffer the pain of ridding myself of this sinful marriage, and, for the sake of the realm, to enter upon another, God-pleasing union I petition the Court of the Holy See to dispose favorably of my self-accusation, and also to consider my willingness to do penance This for all our sake and well being (HENRY *salutes the court with a respectful, yet wily gesture, and exits*)

(*Final TRUMPET BLAST.* ANNE *retires to a couch*)

KATARINA (*In an entirely different tone of voice than before, clear and free*) What I have done, Jane! At last I will act as befits me What I have done 'til now, did not For years now, he has persecuted me according to the principles they call the spirit of the modern age So far I have fought them with their own weapons, with guile against guile, with force against force

JANE That you have, Milady, and everyone admires you for it

KATARINA But now such a course seems far beneath me

JANE Milady! After so much effort you're not weakening?

KATARINA. No, my dear. Do try and understand. Only now will I begin to assert myself.

JANE. What do you intend to do, Milady?

KATARINA. Whenever he fights me with arrogance, I will fight back with humility. When he attacks me with rage, I will counter with cheerfulness. When he aims at me the poisoned arrow of his intellect, I will fortify myself with the wisdom nature has given to us women since the beginning of time.

JANE. I'm afraid I don't understand.

KATARINA. (*Pained.*) Then listen carefully, my dear. A long time ago my King commanded me to dispense with your services, that you might attend—the future Queen.

JANE. No, Milady! That can't be your wish.

KATARINA. It is now! . . . Accept my deepest thanks, Jane Seymour, for all your love and obedience (*Kisses her*) Obey me now for the last time and go to her. (JANE *crosses stage slowly to Right.* KATARINA *pauses before the crucifix.*) Oh Lord, guide me further upon my road, and let me travel it untroubled by the upheaval of time! (*Exits calmly to Left.*)

JANE. (*From Right.*) Ma'am . . .

ANNE. (*Rising from couch.*) Jane! Are you coming to see me?

JANE. To attend you, Ma'am. Those are my orders.

ANNE The King's?

JANE. The Queen's.

ANNE. Oh, it is a good sign.

JANE. Is it, Ma'am?

ANNE Not, Ma'am, Jane! What's the matter with you? Sit down beside me—as my friend. I'm so happy we found each other again. Aren't you?

JANE (*Depressed*) Yes.— (*Compelled.*) No, Anne!

ANNE Yes?—No?

JANE Forgive me! I know I'm not very bright.

ANNE Oh, Jane!

JANE. But I'm not a piece of furniture to be moved

back and forth, from one room to another And—I must tell you, Anne—the Queen .   .

ANNE The Princess of Aragon!

JANE She's so different from what we thought She's so much, much more

ANNE Enough about her . . .

JANE Anne, what you're doing, doesn't it make you feel uneasy?

ANNE What am I doing?

JANE No, not you What the King does, for your sake.

ANNE He turns Europe upside down for my sake That's something marvelous, Jane, something grand

JANE I don't know about that, Anne. But I'm afraid

ANNE You? Of what?

JANE Aren't you afraid?

ANNE (*With deep breath.*) Yes.—But what have you to fear?

JANE This huge castle, Anne. It always makes me feel uneasy All these dim stairways and corridors that are being used day and night Oh, Anne, I'm not cut out for life at court

ANNE What? You, Jane? A Seymour in whose veins flows royal blood? What would you prefer? To be marooned somewhere in the country with an earl?

JANE Oh, yes, Anne, I'd like that· a home in the country with an earl With children, and flocks of sheep, and doves—and to know: this is mine, this I have, and all is well Let there be sun or hail, harvest or failure, birth or death—no strange, sinister being ever intrudes. It is, from God's hand, a good way to live, and a good way to die, when the time comes

ANNE May God grant you your wish I expect something different from Him—except for one thing—

JANE What might that be?

ANNE. I am with child

JANE Oh, Anne! Milady—would God it be a boy

ANNE (*Hard, hostile*) Don't say that! Let the man ask for that! I say would God it be, whether a boy or a girl, a well-formed child, and may its life be blessed with happiness This I say, I, the mother

HENRY. (*Enters with great buoyancy.*) Love of my world, how do you feel?

ANNE The father?

HENRY (*Notices* JANE.) Seymour here? Good. Pray tell your mistress . . .

ANNE Her mistress released her that she may attend me

HENRY. Well, well! So she has finally given in, (*With sentiment*) the good woman (*To* ANNE) Be so good as to send your lady to summon the woman. I have news   (JANE *exits*)

ANNE The tribunal has reached a verdict?

HENRY (*Carefully*)   good news and bad news

ANNE The tribunal

HENRY The tribunal .   has decided that the King of England is to be commended for the extraordinary sensitivity of conscience, but, (*Comical bitterness*) he need not sorrow any longer. A careful examination of his marriage with Katarina of Aragon has proved it to be above reproach.

ANNE (*With a vicious laugh.*) Your tribunal! Now I'm anxious to hear the good news.

HENRY. You know me, Anne! A stroke of fate that deprives lesser men of their reason, it only sharpens my wits . .

ANNE Go on . .

HENRY. I've been thinking, and (*Places finger tip to nose*) suddenly it became clear to me. If the Pope is unable to respect the God-aroused agitation of my conscience, then he can't possibly be enlightened in Christ.

ANNE Go on . . .

HENRY. I couldn't go on I couldn't. All I could do was put my trust in God And, lo,—He enlightened me. He ordered me to ease my anguish by liberating my people from the tyranny of the Roman bishop.

ANNE. To ease your anguish by liberating your people, your God has called upon you for that?

HENRY. You doubt it?

ANNE. No! I know your God, and I will praise Him!

HENRY. Yes, be happy, Anne. This is the hour! My

Archbishop has proved his piety already by agreeing to perform the sacraments of marriage, to please God, and for our enjoyment.

ANNE For our enjoyment, and to please God

HENRY. (*Leads* ANNE *to the cross, where they kneel. ORGAN. a short modulation*) I, Henry Tudor, King of England, take you, Anne Boleyn, to be my only wife and promise that I will love you and keep you unto death. So help me God! (*ORGAN concludes. They rise, and* HENRY *kisses* ANNE) And now, my wife, and soon to be my Queen, I commend you to seek rest, for the heir's sake! (*He escorts her a few steps to rear, then she continues alone into darkness.*)

(KATARINA *enters from Left.*)

HENRY. (*Plants himself in front of her*) Katarina of Aragon. We hereby inform you that you are not, as we believed for so many years, lawfully wed to us.

KATARINA. Our marriage has been approved by the tribunal . . .

HENRY. Not the head of the Church of England .   .

KATARINA The Church of England?

HENRY. The King!

KATARINA The Holy Father commands obedience even from the King

HENRY Not any longer! The bishops of England have requested us to protect the realm from the caprice of the Roman bishop. Under pain of death, the people are not to obey the Vatican, but are to recognize in their anointed King the sole head of the Anglican Church, and the immediate representative of God on earth.

KATARINA I can't believe it! I can't believe that at a time when our church is threatened by Lutheran heresy, you would lead these souls away from the care of the Holy Father.

HENRY. I take their souls under my care, to protect them from the Lutheran pestilence, and from the Roman!

KATARINA. Who are you—I ask you, man, who are you

to take it upon yourself to destroy the covenant which
the Saviour sealed with His blood? Who are you?
Lucifer?

HENRY (*At first, staggered.*) Who am I? (*Savors the
idea, pauses, then rises radically into proclamation*) I
shall tell you who I am I am the man of the modern
times, the man who frees his senses and becomes fully
conscious of the gift God has presented to him, the all-
powerful reason. I am the man who crosses vast oceans
and discovers, beyond the oceans, new continents I am
the man who is not afraid to question nature, and to
demand answers, one after another I am the man whose
genius penetrates heaven and views the earth as, contrary
to the Scriptures, it is whirling around the sun in endless
space Yes, I understand all that really is, be it the way
of the world, or the way of the heart, be it the song of
the stars, or—the voice of conscience

KATARINA (*Before the crucifix.*) Oh, my Saviour, I
beseech Thee, protect Thy Kingdom on earth

HENRY That is blasphemy! Away from Him! (*He
pulls her away from the cross, and she falls to the
ground.*) You shall not come between us, woman!
(*Jumps on the base of the crucifix.*) In His name it is
done! Who doubts me, doubts Him. But where He is
denied, I will take His side, I, the Defender of the
Faith! (*With that he spreads his arms, blotting out the
figure on the cross*)

KATARINA (*Looking up from floor*) Oh, my Saviour,
I can't see Thee any more I can only see man, and he
has already crucified himself (*On her knees*) My Saviour, I see it is the will of the Father to let man inherit
the earth . just once, for one brief earth-hour I can
see that hour in the splendor of its high minutes and in
the horror of its last seconds, and I bow my head before
the wisdom of the Almighty, whom it has pleased, to let
this come to pass (KATARINA *rises, comes to front Left
Faraway tone of voice*) And as far as you're concerned
Henry of England, how does it begin for you this new
age? (HENRY *does what* KATARINA *describes*) You drop

your pose, man of the modern times! You touch your
forehead. No, it's not the plague that makes you break
out in sweat. It's the evil of your new existence. You
have overcome the fear of God, but with your freedom
you have won anxiety. And what happens further, Henry
of England? (JANE *appears.*) One day Jane appears and
informs you that a child has been born to you.

HENRY. A son!

JANE. A daughter!

HENRY. (*Crying out.*) No! God can't do this to me!

JANE. (*Stolidly.*) Your Majesty, it cannot be changed

HENRY (*Embittered, contemptuously.*) It is a daughter. Well, call her . . . Elizabeth!

KATARINA. (*Quietly*) Queen Elizabeth—greatest ruler
England has ever known. And further?

HENRY. I must have a son! (JANE *attempts to leave
Strangely*) Seymour! (JANE *returns*) Come closer!
(JANE *trembles under* HENRY'S *examining gaze.*)

KATARINA. And in that moment you have already
reached your verdict about the other.

CURTAIN

ACT TWO

Left foreground, in dim light, ANNE BOLEYN *in Tower.*

ANNE BOLEYN Damp masonry, foul air, and a hard
bedstead—that's the reverse side of the new life And
when the sun rises, my head on the block Why?
(*Shrieks*) Can they do this to me? By what right? I am
a woman as any other—more beautiful, perhaps, than
others, and God knows, I was haughty. But can they
slay me for that? Then why? Because he so desires, the
despot who crossed my path And when I kneel down
in the first light of dawn, I shall imagine that he is
standing above me, wielding the axe You are above me,
Henry Tudor! I am yours today as in the glorious days
when you and I defied an entire world, to win our lives
for all times Now you permit them to cut me down like
a crippled horse What have I really done that you
should let this happen? Not, as you said, committed
adultery That is not true! I did fail you by not bearing
you the son and heir, and that is wicked, I realize now
For good is, what pleases you, wicked, what proves
troublesome Thus I stood with you against your wife,
thus you now stand against me It is only just, Henry
Tudor! It is like everything you choose to do It is
meant for the best.

(ANNE BOLEYN *remains in the dim light, deeply ab-
sorbed in thought* CANDLELIGHT *to the right*
JANE SEYMOUR *kneels beside a bed standing parallel
to footlights, and prays in a subdued voice*)

JANE SEYMOUR Holy Mary, Mother of God, intercede
for her Mary, most blessed among women, intercede . . .
HENRY (*Raises himself in bed, behind* JANE) Jane!
What the devil! It's two more hours 'til daybreak.
JANE. Two more hours for her.

HENRY. For whom?

JANE You know very well.

HENRY. (*Upright*.) Criminals must die, so the good people can sleep without fear Come back to sleep

JANE. The woman is in the Tower, waiting for the executioner How can I sleep?

HENRY. I can

JANE No! You count every stroke of the bell, too . .

HENRY If I can't sleep it's because you're not next to me. I need the warmth of your body, woman It's my life's blood

JANE You are afraid!

HENRY. Me? Afraid? (*Laughs hoarsely*) Afraid of what? Yes, that too little sleep might endanger my child in your womb. Come under the blanket, woman!

JANE Henry, you prohibited me to intervene for her, but I can't help myself I beseech you .

HENRY Oh, my God, to what depth have morals sunk in my realm if an honorable woman intercedes for a wanton!

JANE She was your wife

HENRY I had the marriage annulled, therefore she was not my wife! Can't you understand that?

JANE No But if that holds true, then—I mean—since I've been sharing your bed for months now, I, too, am a wanton

HENRY Wrong It was my royal obligation to test your fertility This being the case, we can now be joined in holy matrimony, and thus sanctify our actions. You are my wife!

JANE Does that seem right to you?

HENRY Seem right? It is right!

JANE (*Firm*) No! No, it isn't right!

HENRY What is important is how one interprets right And God blesses a suitable interpretation (*Slaps his thigh*) The King and his beloved hold a humanistic discussion I had no idea you were good for that, too—

JANE. Henry, save the woman who was the only love of your life!

HENRY. (*Screams*) Not another word about her!
(*Forced.*) I said we hold a humanistic discussion, and
we will! (*While, on the other side of the bed, he slips
into trousers, shoes and robe*) I can't help her, even if
I were so disposed She was condemned after a fair trial,
and it's my duty as sovereign to see to it that the verdict
is carried out (*Calls carelessly*) Come drink! Yes, I
would have to be afraid should I ever neglect my duties
(*He has rounded the bed and stops, wiping perspiration
from his brow While helping* JANE *into a robe and
leading her to front.*) So you see, you needn't worry, my
good soul Come, drink, and be merry!

JANE. How can I ever be merry again?

(ANNE BOLEYN *paces up and down in a very limited
space, slowly at first, then faster.*)

HENRY I tell you, ere the cock crows you'll be laughing

JANE. (*Shrilly*) Laughing? Ere the cock crows? Ere
the ax falls and the bell tolls?

HENRY. I say to you, the living who are without guilt,
to you who have the man and the child for the man, you
will laugh! Now, ask another one of your dear, silly
questions.

JANE I don't know any.

HENRY. You don't know any?

JANE (*Tortured.*) No.

HENRY No more questions? There's nothing that you
don't know? Ha, I'm laughing already. And so are you!

JANE. I'm not.

HENRY (*Viciously.*) I insist we have a humanistic
discussion

JANE (*Seizing upon it.*) What is humanistic?

HENRY The learned conduct after the example of the
ancients, as it is so splendidly practised today

JANE What's it good for?

HENRY. To act wisely, and always to consider the
humane.

JANE Consider the humane? Then there won't be any more unjust trials . . .

HENRY And no more wars.

JANE (*Doubtingly*) No wars?!

HENRY The truth will spread among the peoples of the earth, and once more they will form a peaceful community under God.

JANE. (*Screams*) There!

(ANNE BOLEYN *stops her rapid walk and drops to her knees.*)

HENRY What is it?

JANE. Listen! The bell strikes four. Now she has only one more hour.

HENRY (*Shuddering*) Why should that concern us?

JANE. Oh, if we could only perceive what it must feel like, when one must die by our hand!

(ANNE BOLEYN *prays, at first desperately, but gradually she gains more control over herself*)

HENRY Come drink and don't grieve, my good girl You mustn't for the sake of the child you're carrying. Come, drink! He shall get used to the golden juice, the lad! The earlier the better! (*Calls*) Have them make music! .   Music does for the mood what a blanket does for the body. They shall cover us with music! . . . Now—what were we talking about? Ah, it's such a joy to carry on a discussion with you! I promise, you'll be laughing ere the cock crows!

JANE. In this purgatory?

HENRY. (*Threateningly*) What did you say?

JANE. I'm suffering purgatory right now.

HENRY. The Popes invented purgatory—for Shrove money. I have done away with this exploitation of the people, . . . and raised the taxes. (*MUSIC sets in*) . . . Ah, what lovely rhythms Did you know, my girl, that I'm also a musician? I've enhanced many of my own verses with delicate melodies.

JANE. (*Somewhat affected by the wine.*) Just like the Emperor Nero He did that too!

HENRY. (*Smugly.*) Only he was a heathen, while I'm the immediate representative of God on earth!

JANE (*Surrendering*) Oh, you're a wonder, my Henry.

HENRY. (*Over her.*) My wife! (*Slaps her behind*) Beautiful you're not, but what joy and comfort to your sovereign's worldly appetites A pity I must deny my urge to take you now, you shrine, bearing England's future.

JANE Henry—if you want your child to grow within a happy woman

HENRY. I damn well expect that!

JANE Then grant me one wish

HENRY. Anything, unless it violates my good conscience

JANE If your conscience prevents you from sparing Anne's life . . . it's possible that she is an adulteress . . . and she certainly is haughty

HENRY That she was

JANE . . then I beg you, do not let the other one spend her days in sorrow and need Go to Katarina, make peace with her (HENRY *moves away from her with a groan*) She was a dear and wise mistress to me, and she was your loyal wife Provide for her and for your daughter.

HENRY (*Takes a deep swallow*) This my conscience does not permit I, soon to be your husband, should visit the woman who for twenty years has lived with me in a shameful concubinage? How can I do this to you? Ask for something else.

(ANNE BOLEYN *looks up as the reddish DAWN rises, gets up and arranges attire and hair.*)

JANE (*Also seeing the dawn, screams*) Free me from that!

HENRY. From what?

JANE. There! The red above the windows! It's the dawn No, it's Anne's blood. I beg you, make it go away! Make it go away!

HENRY. I can't bear to see you suffer. (*Calls*) Have them light torches! many torches! (*One piece of MUSIC ends, ANOTHER begins. The background becomes a raging sea of FLAMES*) There, you see! It has disappeared in the fire of the torches. (*Fearfully decreeing.*) It is no more!

(ANNE BOLEYN *walks slowly, with heavy steps, passing between* HENRY *and* JANE, *into the bright light in the background.*)

HENRY. (*Shuddering.*) Why are you so quiet, my dear? (*Noisily.*) Come, let us drink to Edward, our son!

JANE. (*Outburst*) And if it isn't a son?

HENRY. What?

JANE. (*Trembling.*) Will you have me tried, too?

HENRY Why?

JANE. (*Confused*) Because it won't be a boy, if it isn't a boy . . .

HENRY (*Upright; indulgently*) What an absurd notion that a man should be angry at his wife for not presenting him with the heir he desires Pray tell, is it your doing, how nature mixes the juices in your belly? . . . No, Jane Seymour, if you'll be my faithful wife, as I think you will be, then we'll have a wonderful marriage And, indeed, it would be the devil's handiwork if I, with my caliber, couldn't sire a few sons.

JANE (*Wildly throwing herself into his arms*) Yes, that's how it shall be, my terrible husband and King.

HENRY You see, now you're happy again Didn't I promise you, you'll be laughing

JANE I'm not laughing But now I'm glad I've been denied her vain beauty

HENRY. It is well And, by God, we shall enjoy our lives We well deserve it, being such good people and so full of love. (*Sings to the music like a child that is fear-stricken.*) Dance with me, woman! Today you still may, and it strengthens your loins. (JANE *dances with him, completely abandoning herself, and they laugh in a panicky daring. Suddenly a deep stroke of a BELL sounds, and the MUSIC stops abruptly* JANE *continues laughing in a sensuous outburst Crossing himself*) Why are you laughing, woman?

JANE. Because I'm happy, I, who am without guilt, I who have the man and the child for the man, I, the living, I, Jane Seymour!

HENRY. (*Turns from her with horror, drops to his knees, whimpers*) Anne! Anne Boleyn! Oh,—what have I done! (JANE, *with a sob, throws herself across the bed Continues to himself*) You companion of my great mission, in the whole world there's no other like you, nor will there ever be You joy of my senses How could I do this to you?! It is too horrible to contemplate that your head, whose every gaze and kiss and speech was the delight of my days, is pale now and severed from the body which was the delight of my nights It had to be, I had no choice. How can I ever atone for it?   But, how can I make it up to you? . . Yes, upon my word, I will do what this good woman asked I will visit Katarina, and I will care for her. It is an oath! (*Grimly. He rises and exits into the darkness in the rear*)

JANE. Lord! Lord! Lord! Take the poor woman unto you, and take her graciously! . . . But, oh, my God! . what is it about this man that he destroys every woman he ever touches?

(*Candle and torch LIGHTS off. Clear daylight.* KATARINA *or* ARAGON *in a light dress*)

KATARINA (*Serene and pleasant*) It has been three months since he vowed to visit me For three months he continues to hem and haw One day Jane enters confinement And suddenly he is in a hurry to keep his word (*She sits down*) I await him in the garden He mustn't see the poverty of my lodgings. Out here I am better equipped than inside. The October day sparkles all gold and blue —Why does he leave his retinue behind? Ah— he is ashamed of his human stirrings —There! He knocks at the gate and bellows because no one comes to open it What sort of an estate do you think I maintain? I have one girl and a maid, and they are busy with the laundry You need only press down the latch! But it never occurs to you that the gate is unlocked You knock again, in such a rage that your fist crashes through the rotten wood, your boot pushes after and thus, my gallant knight, you storm the open castle!

HENRY'S VOICE (*From nearby.*) Hello there! Is no one about?

KATARINA (*Subdued voice*) Yes No one

HENRY (*Enters, stops directly in front of* KATARINA *and shouts*) Hey! Katarina!

KATARINA. Look here, I'm not hiding, and yet you can't find me You can't hear me, because you're too noisy You can't see me, because you're much too enlightened . . Never, in all your life, will you discover what you're searching for, Henry Tudor

HENRY. Hey! Is this place enchanted?

KATHRYN HOWARD (*Enters*) God's greetings, Sir What is it you wish?

HENRY. (*Pacified and pleased by her looks*) It is enchanted

KATARINA (*Aside.*) Of course; for a doe you have not lost the scent. (*Remains waiting*)

HENRY God's greetings, my child (*Enjoys her looks*)

KATHRYN (*Recognizes him, shocked*) Your Majesty.

HENRY You know me?

KATHRYN The princess had a gold coin with your image

HENRY Had a gold coin? I see But here she has a treasure far more valuable than gold. Who are you? How old? Still a virgin?

KATHRYN. Kathryn Howard, Your Majesty.

HENRY. No!

KATHRYN. Indeed, Your Majesty. Earl Edmund's daughter, if it pleases.

HENRY. It pleases.

KATHRYN. (*Notices* KATARINA) Your Majesty, the princess—

HENRY. Let's not disturb her. Well, well, a blossom from Norfolk's tree. (*Slyly shaking a threatening finger.*) I suppose, sharing his confounded leanings to Rome?

KATHRYN. (*With lowered head, slyly.*) Not necessarily, Your Majesty, not necessarily.

HENRY. I like you

KATHRYN. The princess—

HENRY. Are you turning a cold shoulder because I didn't recognize you? Don't make me unhappy!

KATHRYN. Even the moon finds it impossible to know every star.

HENRY. A sublime answer!

KATHRYN. The princess awaits Your Majesty. (*Points to* KATARINA. HENRY *grunts angrily, and* KATHRYN *retires discreetly.*)

HENRY. (*Plants himself in front of* KATARINA, *and hardly looking at her, recites mechanically and surly.*) Katarina of Aragon: greetings! We wish to inform you that in paternal care for our subjects, while engaged in the inspection of convents, mines and asylums for the needy, we have also decided, to inquire after your well-being. We have already discovered that you suffer a shortage of gold, and, by our own experience, have found that the entrance gate is in need of repair. We are willing to alleviate such sundry needs, within set limits, of course. We will also visit your daughter. There is no need for you to express your gratitude. We are merely discharging our Royal obligations. (*Suddenly in an intimate tone of voice*) How did you come upon Kathryn Howard?

KATARINA (*In a beautiful, rich and gay voice.*) I am grateful, for your kindness, yet I hardly require it, as I have enough to cover all my needs

HENRY. (*Looks at her in amazement*) Katarina!

Your voice! And the way you look! What has happened
to you? (*Quickly aims at her with his finger.*) You have
a lover.

KATARINA. No.

HENRY. Then what is it?

KATARINA. Perhaps—freedom.

HENRY Freedom? You, too?

KATARINA Yes, but it's different from yours—less
boisterous, less forced

HENRY But you're imprisoned behind these walls

KATARINA I can't see the walls—only the sky above
and the bountiful leaves—I was imprisoned in Madrid,
and in London. Here I can live and do as I please. I'm
grateful to you, Henry—

HENRY. (*Heartfelt*) I'm grateful to you for receiving
me like this I came here, in a dark mood, on an unavoidable visit, and it is a glorious day!

KATARINA. It is good to sit out here. (*They sit down.*)
You asked about Kathryn?

HENRY (*Lively*) Yes

KATARINA She's my god-child, and an orphan. 'Til
now she has been living at Norfolk Castle, with her
aunt

HENRY She has a quick tongue, half humility, half
wit Sweet—sour Appeals to me greatly.

KATARINA She's well-read, and she recites poetry
beautifully, but she'll never get married.

HENRY (*Naively*) I'm not looking for a wife.

KATARINA Why should you!

HENRY I have a good one, who is just facing her
proudest hour. But, should I need one, today it would
have to be a Lutheran

KATARINA (*Still gay and easy.*) A Lutheran? You—
the Defender of the Faith?

HENRY The winds of statesmanship blow from many
different directions It seems opportune now to seek a
connection with the German princes.

KATARINA The heretic princes?

HENRY. In order to defend the faith, as it is guarded by England—

KATARINA. Oh yes, England—'

HENRY. I must view the situation matter-of-factly

KATARINA. Matter-of-factly? What's that? I have never heard that expression before.

HENRY. It's something new. But it has a great future.

KATARINA. But what is it? Is it a matter or a fact?

HENRY Well, for example: if a wife is unable to give her husband an heir— No, that's not quite the right example—

KATARINA. Oh, but yes—it is! If a woman is unable to give her husband the heirs he requires, it's a matter of fact.

HENRY. Yes.

KATARINA. But, tell me: which is the matter, which is the fact?

HENRY. (*Perplexed.*) I didn't invent the phrase.

KATARINA. (*Elegantly.*) I'll have Kathryn bring you wine, to refresh your wits.

HENRY. (*Laughing.*) Your wit is as refreshed as your skin, and as clear as your eyes.

KATARINA It is only the light of the October day, the reflection of the sun in the autumn leaves—

HENRY. (*Gently.*) The reflection of the sun it might well be.

KATARINA. (*Happy by his mood.*) Oh, Henry, you, too, have changed.

HENRY (*Blustery.*) As I said before: Your garden is enchanted.

KATARINA. My garden is a garden as any other. Your world out there is enchanted.

HENRY. What is it about my world, Katarina?

KATARINA. Yes, what is it that a simple garden can free us from its curse . . .

HENRY. I feel I can talk with you in confidence, dearest . . .

KATARINA (*Carefully.*) Then tell me, Henry . . .

the age that you proclaimed in the name of reason
what is the matter with it? Look at the first few centuries, and all you see are cruel wars, all waged in the
name of faith Tell me, where does that leave reason?

HENRY You see, dearest, Luther fastened ninety-five
theses to the gate of modern times But with a hammer
far more powerful than his, three more were nailed to
the door. They are: gold . . . state . . . power

KATARINA. What has that?— Oh, now I understand.
These three are the matters of fact

HENRY. Precisely.

KATARINA. Then how can wars be waged in the name
of faith?

HENRY Faith is an important factor in our age. You
said so yourself.

KATARINA Faith is the creative force of all ages But
with all these factors working for you, why have you
failed to produce a new and better existence?

HENRY We have produced something new. the
triumph of materialism.

KATARINA (*Shattered*) Out of a great need for God—
gold, state and power? That's monstrous!

HENRY God's ways are miraculous

KATARINA Oh, I'm not as pious as you, Henry I
can't understand that. So the princes used faith merely
as a pretext to wage wars?

HENRY. What a frivolous thought! No, by heeding the
call of their conscience, they also, according to God's
will, turned it into a profitable venture

KATARINA Now I understand! The needs of the conscience as the basis of profit This has happened to us
once before, hasn't it, Henry?

HENRY I didn't invent conscience.

KATARINA. No, your enemy Luther did that But you
were the one who so cleverly blended the two: conscience,
and the matter of fact— the decent intention and the
decent profit

HENRY When I struggled with you for our marriage—
that was honest, Katarina.

KATARINA That's precisely what I mean That you could do it honestly, that was the accomplishment! Hypocrites have always existed But to sanctify every desire, every deed, and now, every action of state—not by lying, as Machiavelli suggested—oh, no, but to sanctify it honestly, as the true call of your conscience—that is new, Henry, and for that you can take all the credit.

HENRY. (*Defeated for a moment, then a brilliant turnabout.*) It pleases me enormously that you should be the first to recognize my place in history. But, tell me, dearest. how come you know me that well?

KATARINA. (*With a mild smile*) I studied you for half my life, as a sick person studies his sickness.

HENRY There! Now you're smiling again But enough about politics It's such a dirty business (KATARINA *attempts to reply*) Please, dearest, I beg you, recognize in these centuries the great forward sweep of the intellect

KATARINA. (*Pained*) I see it, Henry, and I admire it

HENRY (*Enthusiastic*) No! You!

KATARINA. Oh, yes! I truly admire it! But the people tell it as the story of Doctor Faustus who enters into a pact with Satan in order to obtain unlimited knowledge, the most beautiful woman, and the greatest power. Have you heard that fable?

HENRY. Yes (*Suddenly*) I shall tell you what I think I think that I, Henry Tudor, am Faustus in the stage of power . .

KATARINA (*Amused*) Because you've already done away with the first two stages? The quest for knowledge—and done away with the most beautiful woman? (HENRY *twitches*) No, Henry, you're not Faustus. You're Satan's peddler

HENRY. (*With humor.*) I suppose I had that coming to me. And do you think that, in the end, Satan will push us, too, into eternal damnation?

KATARINA. Why Satan? You'll manage it yourself.

HENRY. Unless, of course, we find the road back to the old knowledge. Eh?

KATARINA Yes, Henry.

HENRY. (*Sarcastic*) The knowledge of Augustine and Thomas?

KATARINA The old knowledge, Henry, is not what once was, but what will always be Many are aware of its wisdom who have never been to school. A farmer, for instance, whose simple spirit is deeply rooted in the soil.

HENRY. That may well be, but we're not that simple.

KATARINA No You have learned to cross oceans in daring curiosity, and where you searched for India, you conquered a new world The new knowledge is to keep crossing the ocean again and again, and to keep forever searching for the new beyond the ocean. But the old knowledge—is the ocean!

KATHRYN HOWARD (*Enters excitedly.*) Forgive me, Your Majesty! A message has arrived Your Majesty has a healthy son.

HENRY. (*With deepest emotion, quietly.*) Oh, tell me once again, you lovely voice Sing it out once more: Majesty, Majesty, Majesty, it is a son! I, Henry, by the Grace of God, King of England, the eighth of my name, son of the victorious Henry Tudor, I, by God's great Grace, I have a son!

KATARINA. Henry . . . I'm happy that Providence has at last granted you this.

HENRY. (*Rising, sincere*) Thank you, dearest! May heaven preserve your happy disposition. For everything else I will provide generously. (*To* KATHRYN.) And you, too, charming messenger, accept my thanks. (*He kisses her*) And now back to London!

KATARINA. (*To* KATHRYN.) How is the mother? Did the messenger say?

KATHRYN. (*With a fearful look at* HENRY.) The mother is in danger.

HENRY. The child's baptism takes place come Wednesday.

KATARINA. Baptism without the mother?

HENRY With the mother, of course

KATARINA The mother is in danger

HENRY Wednesday is the day my astrologer selected

KATARINA The mother is in danger Allow her to remain in childbed

HENRY. Custom demands that she bring the child to me

KATARINA Henry! Man! Listen· to force her to get up may prove fatal.

HENRY Only by handing the child to me can she demonstrate to the world that everything which I have done, was necessary, and for the good of the realm.

KATARINA And if this—play-acting costs her life?

HENRY. God can not want that to happen

KATARINA But suppose it does?

HENRY (*Piously*) Then it is obviously God's intention that I shall take a Lutheran One has already been offered to me, the daughter of the Duke of Cleves Not the youngest any more, but easy to look at, as Master Holbein's portrait indicates (*Exits*)

KATARINA (*Grandly*) Oh, merciful Providence, I beg thee withhold the thunderbolt this insolent spirit deserves a thousandfold

(*LIGHTS change.*)

JANE SEYMOUR (*Rises from her bed with great difficulty*) I know you mean well, my gentle ladies, I know the doctors have prohibited it But my husband insists, and not without reason Therefore I must do it, and be it only to atone for my laughter when my friend was put to death (*Takes child from crib*) Come, you tender fruit of my heart, I must take you to your father, the all-powerful King, that I may offer you to him before the people And that he may offer you to our God And then, good-by, my son—good-by, and become a good human being and Christian

(JANE SEYMOUR *walks slowly with the child to the center of the stage. Colorful LIGHTS. St Paul's Cathedral. BELLS.* HENRY *walks toward her with a ceremonial stride from the rear. When he arrives by* JANE *he runs his hand over her hair, and kisses her ceremoniously. Humbly she hands the child over to him. He takes it with a smile, and turns toward the rear, puts it down and baptizes it. While he picks it up again,* JANE *collapses.* HENRY *steps over her prostrate form and shows the child, holding it high, and his face glows with pride and satisfaction.*)

CURTAIN

ACT THREE

*The port of Dover A winter STORM rages Royal
FANFARE Henry and Kathryn Howard enter*

HENRY. Stand over there, my child And recite in a
loud voice, otherwise the storm will drown out my
ingenious sonnet

KATHRYN (*With chattering teeth*) Your Majesty,
I'm afraid your verses will freeze on my lips

HENRY Have as much courage as the German maiden
Anna who braves the ice-bound channel to sail into my
arms (*Another fanfare announces the arrival of the
boat*) Sound like a trumpet, my little oboe! Europe
comes to me!

(ANNA OF CLEVES *arrives, and curtsies from the distance HENRY responds with grave reverence
ANNA'S face is veiled*)

KATHRYN (*Curtsies before ANNA, and, shivering in
the cold, shouts the poem into the storm, fully empha-
sizing the crass dilettantism of Henry's verses*)
　　He, whose yearning heart first saw your smile
　　On the portrait fashioned by the master's hand
　　Proffers nuptial greetings on his Isle
　　To you, O handsome lady from Germanland
But I, chosen harbinger of his love, echo these words
set down by my King— (KATHRYN *curtsies again, and
takes her place behind* HENRY)

ANNA OF CLEVES (*Removes her veil She has an extremely homely face with a flat nose Resolutely she
begins to recite her prepared speech*) Exalted Majesty
of England! I thank Your Grace with profound gratitude
for the tender and loving emotions which Your Grace's
peculiar genius has so beautifully expressed in this
poem I thank you in all humility, but I can not help

experiencing great pride that you, the powerful King and Master of the world—

HENRY (*Shocked at the sight of her, he retreats at first, then immensely consternated, he twists and turns forward, rubs his eyes, looks at* ANNA *over his shoulder, and heaves a deep sigh*) No, gracious Providence, no! (*Flees, while whispering irritably to* KATHRYN) Be kind to me, Kathryn Do you know the painting of my German bride? (*Deeply embarrassed,* KATHRYN *shakes her head*) I know the painting—but that I don't know!

KATHRYN (*In a futile effort*) Perhaps the seasickness—

HENRY The seasickness! Since when does that ailment twist and flatten the nose? Maybe it's the bridesmaid! (*Fervently*) Oh, Lord, let it be the bridesmaid! (*Faces* ANNA *again.*)

ANNA (*Makes a fresh start*) —that you, the powerful King and Master of the world, have chosen me to be your loving bride, and that I, in tenderness and loyalty and desired fertility—

HENRY (*Calls to rear*) Saddle my horse!

KATHRYN Your Majesty! Your Majesty!

HENRY (*Cuts her off with a gesture of his hands*) I don't want that! It can't be It isn't It's never been!

KATHRYN Your Majesty, all Europe is watching you!

HENRY (*Crushed*) Europe Yes It looks at me with a German cow eyes She's Europa, and I'm her bull (*Calls lamentably*) Leave the horse! (*Aside*) I've saddled myself (*To* ANNA, *with forced courtesy*) Continue, my dearest, I meant to say, don't continue It pains me to see you shiver with cold Come into the bridal pavilion, and warm yourself by the fire, and have some punch We need it! (*He gestures* ANNA *to the Right, walking behind her, watching her walk with a grim gaze* KATHRYN *exits with* ANNA'S *cloak* HENRY *discards his, and settles with* ANNA *before a fireplace, and fills two glasses with punch Sour*) Welcome, Anna of Cleves, my cherished bride

ANNA (*Boiling with rage*) To your good health, cherished groom (*They drink heartily.*)

HENRY Was the crossing very unpleasant?

ANNA. Oh—then it was only the boat that rocked under my feet, now it's my entire world. (*Empties her glass with one draught*)

HENRY (*As he watches her drink his respect for her grows*) We should have reined our hearts desire 'til spring

ANNA Our hearts were all too desirous to—anger the Pope.

HENRY (*Sighs*) How right you are! (*Embarrassed silence. To say something.*) Anne!—I already had one with that name. (ANNA *cries out horror-stricken.*) What's the matter?

ANNA. (*Pulls herself together.*) I'm surprised. I carefully traced your family's genealogy. I don't remember anyone with that name.

HENRY. Because I ordered it erased. (*Sadly looking into the glass*) She was beautiful—but contemptible. (*Looks at* ANNA.) You, without a doubt, are—virtuous.

ANNA. Several character references have been submitted to Your Majesty's ambassador, also a medical affidavit attesting to my virginity.

HENRY. It's all right I meant to say—

ANNA. You meant to say. virtuous—but ugly!

HENRY. By all the martyr's tears, how can such a thought even occur to someone as stately as you! For example· your ears are of a lovely shape—like sea shells

ANNA. (*Snaps at him*) Are you suggesting that my ears can as readily arouse your senses as the eyes and the lips of a beautiful woman? Not to mention other—

HENRY (*Bursts out*) How I wish I could tear out Holbein's eyes, and plant them into my face, to see you as he sees you!

ANNA Now I have it! My portrait by Holbein—

HENRY No, no! Not for a moment do I consider the portrait flattering Just to the contrary. the original overshadows it—overshadows it Just—that you, as you materialized before me in flesh and blood—are different. Do you understand? Different! Your abundant charms are – how can I explain—

ANNA You don't have to.

HENRY —are—so God wills,—just not the sort to arouse my stubborn blood

ANNA. (*Strong*) In short· I don't appeal to you, you don't want me

HENRY In short· You don't appeal to me, but I do want you For, make no mistake, the marriage must take place!

ANNA. (*Sobbingly*) You want me to become your wife, even if you don't care for me?

HENRY Did I ever say that? Did I ever say that I don't care for you? I care for you very much.

ANNA That's not true (*Drinks.*)

HENRY. (*Beats his breast*) May I never find bliss! For example· The way you empty a glass in one draught, —magnificent, my dear, absolutely magnificent That in itself is almost reason enough for our marriage!

ANNA (*Wretched*) I'm from the Rhineland Only there we drink our wine cold—not like soup.

HENRY *Mille pardons!* And then your mouth-piece,— it's true the creator has been somewhat remiss in making it enticing to my lips, but He certainly endowed it with a glib tongue. Pleases me enormously, my dear. I can't begin to tell you how much. You're a stalwart woman, eh? With a resolute view for—facts?

ANNA. (*Still tearful*) That's true.

HENRY. Have some more punch! You can take it, eh?

ANNA. (*Determinedly.*) I can take it!

HENRY. (*Very pleasant*) Obviously. Now, then: let's think this out sensibly. The marriage must take place You agree, don't you?

ANNA. Yes.

HENRY. All right. Then we shall submit stoically to the inevitable. Allow me, however, that in this unavoidable marriage, I—how shall I put it?—renounce once and for all the bodily comfort which you're certainly capable of offering (ANNA *sadly lowers her head*) That you, and your body's intimate desires shall lie untilled Could you get resigned to that? Could you? (ANNA *nods subserviently*) You won't mind? (ANNA *shakes her head* HENRY, *hurt*) You won't mind?!

ANNA Sire, until my thirtieth year I've persistently done without the pleasures which, as I hear, the man can offer the woman The more hopefully, of course, I looked forward to enjoying now, to the fullest, your gigantic masculinity

HENRY You're touching my heart.

ANNA But if you want to deny me your bed, well, then I shall be content with throne and table

HENRY (*Slaps his thigh*) Good girl!

ANNA For the long hours of the night when I—as you so tenderly put it,—shall lie untilled, I have the inspiring writings of Doctor Luther   .

HENRY (*Sour*) For that he's well applied But let me tell you, for your comfort, my dear· According to Catholic doctrine, abstinence in marriage is a virtue of the highest order, and almost sufficient reason for beatification

ANNA For a heretic, too?

HENRY At least it will lessen your torments in hell. If you'd only stop and think for a moment how other men, by brutally and lustfully demanding from their wives carnal satisfaction, prevent these poor creatures from attaining eternal salvation, then you'll have to admit that in that respect, at least, you have made an exceptionally advantageous marriage

ANNA (*With grim humor*) You have a damned sly way of shaping life to suit you You treat it like a pillow (*Indicates with a motion of her hands*) that you pommel into place

HENRY (*Slaps her thigh*) Well said, sister! You understand me! What a pity your nose isn't as straight as your speech "Like a pillow"! Yes, that's how I am, true to St Paul's saying "Those who love God, must serve all things to the best " I love God!

ANNA Good for you, devout man.

HENRY. And thus, my cherished bride, we shall keep our marriage paulistic praise the spirit, and be contemptuous of the flesh! And now, to seal the bargain, I must kiss your thin, but impudent lips.

(As ANNA *nears him, LIGHTS change.)*

HENRY *(After a pause)* In the sixth month of our most harmonious misalliance, I inform you cordially that our days together are numbered (ANNA *jumps up with a terrified scream)* What's the matter?

ANNA Sire—you have a favorite method of dealing with excess wives

HENRY What an absurd notion! Why should I do this to my virtuous German sister, my able boon companion?

ANNA. *(Again at his side)* Then how?

HENRY Since you, our dear wife, according to God's will, have remained barren—

ANNA Totally unexpected

HENRY We shall, for the sake of people, declare our marriage annulled We grant you the title. Sister of the King, and an estate in the country with an annual income of two thousand pounds

ANNA. Four thousand

HENRY Three thousand—and worth doubly that to a Lutheran, since the money is derived from confiscated convents

ANNA. But—

HENRY. *(Frowning)* What else?

ANNA. Must the King's sister remain faithful to her brother?

HENRY. *(Laughs)* What do you take me for? A

monster? Buy yourself a young and strong earl, and
make the most of it!

ANNA I'll follow your advice to the best of my ability

HENRY Miss nothing

ANNA I said to the best of my ability I'm best able
with—four thousand and two estates

HENRY (*Grabs her enthusiastically*) Ah, you're the
best! The only woman I've ever been able to talk with,
and, because of God's unfathomable will you must have
such a nose I could almost overlook it

ANNA (*Ardent*) Could you?

HENRY I said almost You're trembling?

ANNA I'm a woman, Henry

HENRY (*Perplexed*) Come to the fireplace

ANNA No wooden fire can help our needs (*Exits*)

HENRY (*Greatly perturbed*) What has happened to
me? That I should let a woman slip from my side? My
heart, that infallible compass which invariably indicates
the needs of the moment, has locked itself against her
What went wrong? The heart or—the woman? The
needle or—the nose? Am I getting old? No! Oh, yes, I
am getting old! The gout festers in my leg, and one of
my favorite powers is developing a mind of its own And
I'm beginning to dread being alone Yes, I'm getting old,
and I don't like it one damn bit! It's a horrible sensation
to have passed the peak and to be looking down at the
shadowy exit What is there to be done? By the devil!
I shall follow the dictates of my heart. And the infallible
needle points to the shy being who so valiantly shouted
my verses into the storm. Kathryn Howard! But—can I
love her truly? The Howards are Papists. Well, haven't
I been severely punished for having tried it with a
Lutheran? Is there a better way to atone than to fortify
myself against the Pope with a young Papist in my bed?
My benevolent heart—! It yearns for purification, and
see here· I love the devout maiden! Oh, my heart, you
are so understanding! You proclaim the summer, not
autumn It's Whitsun for Henry Tudor! And before me

spreads a precious harvest! (*Exits pompously to rear*)

(*LIGHTS Right*, KATARINA OF ARAGON *and* KATHRYN HOWARD *in a nun's habit walking to Left*.)

KATHRYN HOWARD Seek refuge from the King—at his court?

KATARINA The court is a labyrinth, in which few know their way about   the widow Parr probably better than most We will find her at this nightly hour in her library   Kate! Kate Parr!

KATE PARR Who is it? Two devout women at this late hour?

KATARINA Kate, this is Kathryn Howard She needs your protection

KATE Is Greenwich visited by the plague?

KATARINA Worse· a marriage-mad King.

KATE Better it were the plague

KATARINA. Can you shelter the girl?

KATE. (*Determined*) Stay with me, Kathryn Howard

KATHRYN. You're very kind, Milady

KATE My friends call me Kate!

KATHRYN (*Grateful*) Kate!

KATARINA. And, Kate you should know. it's not entirely that she doesn't want him She cannot be his wife. Young as she is, she carries a heaven burden.

KATE A secret?

KATARINA If only it were a secret If she became Queen, she'd be at the mercy of extortioners

KATE Oh, you were involved in a Papist conspiracy at Norfolk Castle?

KATHRYN No!

KATE Why the habit?

KATARINA. A disguise

KATE I'm satisfied she needs protection, and it remains to be seen if in this age of enlightenment a girl can be forced to marry the King Oh, how lovely she looks among these old books. a white leaf among so many yellowed ones.

KATHRYN. I wish I were that Then you could place me among the Ten Commandments! He'd never find me there, the Defender of the Faith

KATE. I wouldn't find you there either . . .

KATHRYN. (*Looks at her in astonishment*)

KATARINA Kate studies the new sciences The truly knowing and the truly believing always stand side by side.

(*They rush to front Right. There, in a bright LIGHT, terrifying, stands HENRY, his legs apart, his arms crossed in front of his chest.*)

HENRY. (*Obviously enjoying the women's horror for a moment, he then bursts out laughing.*) Three Katherines! That's too much, even for me. Leave the room—Widow Parr.

KATE. With due respect, Your Majesty! I'm entertaining dear guests,—and is the uninvited guest to chase me away from them?

HENRY. The uninvited, dear guest graciously permits you to return to your room—instead of the Tower.

KATE. (*While exiting, subdued.*) One could meet worse company elsewhere.

HENRY. (*To* KATHRYN.) The—costume is most appealing, my little Kathryn. You will please me many times in the future by putting it on for my pleasure

KATARINA She will not please you in such blasphemous enjoyment nor in any other—

HENRY. She shall! But now, realize your good fortune that I'm such a tender-hearted king. For discovering you here, I could have your ears lopped off But you're finding your sovereign in an indestructibly good mood You see, your sovereign has fallen in love. (*Nears* KATHRYN)

KATARINA (*Steps between them*) Henry, I beg you to leave her be! I say it once more, she must not become your wife. It would be a tragedy for you, as well as for her

HENRY. Tragedy!? For me? In my realm I decide

what constitutes tragedy— Say what you wish. I won't believe you

KATARINA (*Stunned*) You won't believe—me?

HENRY (*Impressed*) Not in this matter, Katarina I know you disdain a lie But, you're a woman, and you were once my wife How could you be free of jealousy now? Don't block my path— (*Advancing to* KATHRYN— *kneels before her*) Kathryn Howard, you royal blossom from an ancient tree, you who combine all the youth and beauty of England, I love you, and I'm willing to place the crown on your head, as is your due (KATHRYN *breaks into tears Rises, stunned*) Why is she upset?

KATARINA Shouldn't she be asked whether or not she wants you?

HENRY Whether she wants me?! Whether she's willing to reign gloriously over all women?! Yes, tell me Are you willing, Kathryn?

KATHRYN (*Compelled*) No

HENRY And why don't you want it?

KATHRYN (*Emphatic*) I should not do you honor

HENRY You're my life!

KATARINA As a lamb is the wolf's life

KATHRYN I know I should not do you honor

HENRY (*Close to her*) Don't worry, my child

KATHRYN I beg Your Majesty not to touch me.

HENRY Only to dispel your fears

KATHRYN. (*Panicky*) Your Majesty, do not touch me!

HENRY What?

KATARINA She's trying to say that in the physical manifestation of Your Majesty—you do not appeal to her—

HENRY (*Disconcerted*) Is that possible?

KATHRYN (*Spontaneous*) Yes

HENRY (*Stunned for a moment, then catching himself*) Girl! Girl! Plato has said that the senses deceive— and it is true I'm more than just a man of flesh I'm a man of reason

KATARINA Then prove it! Let her decide of her own free will!

HENRY. A fine move, Katarina. My respects Very well, I accept the challenge. I'm certain of capturing the white queen. (*To* KATHRYN.) Grant me then, Kathryn Howard, to woo you in all sincerity. Let me name my wedding gift, and describe its true value!

KATARINA (*Sits down.*) Name it, man

HENRY (*Modestly.*) It is the world. I offer it to you as I so magnificently created it

KATHRYN (*Shocked, crosses herself*) Almighty Lord, the world is yours!

HENRY. He has bequeathed it to me, as it is written in Genesis: be fruitful and multiply, and fill the earth and subdue it. He has left it to me as an old peasant leaves the farm to his son. And now listen, girl, to what I've made of it.

KATARINA. Tell us, peasant

HENRY. All the old man left me was a flat clod of earth with a heaven above and a hell below . . .

KATARINA. (*Measured, penetrating polemics, more to* KATHRYN *than* HENRY) In the beginning man created the heavens and the earth.

(KATHRYN, *troubled, whispers the Lord's Prayer, the first lines audibly, the rest during the following.*)

HENRY. While I was establishing order in my father's world I found neither heaven nor hell. But I needed hell as well as I needed heaven, and lo: I discovered both in myself I invented conscience.

KATHRYN. —and lead us not into temptation— (*Stops, looks at* HENRY, *perplexed.*) You invented conscience? I like that.

KATARINA. And man said, "let there be light," and there was light.

KATHRYN. It is written: "You will be like God, and know good and the evil."

KATARINA The serpent said that before the fall of man

KATHRYN. (*Strangely*) It's a comfort to those who survive the fall

HENRY Right, my child, right!—(*Bigoted.*) Make the most of what is written as God's word! Look at me: I've always honored the Lord—while he dwelled among us.

KATARINA (*Penetrating polemics*) —Listen to our peasant: While the old man dwelled among us.

KATHRYN That's horrible! (*Laughs, honestly amused*) How can man pronounce God dead! That's really foolish . . .

HENRY. God ordered me to help mankind, not Him! And,—this I want to tell you. I've set man free.

KATHRYN Only the man?

HENRY. The woman, too, so that she may dispose freely of her life and body—

KATHRYN (*Alarmed*) Dispose freely of her life and body?

HENRY. Yes, dearest, yes!

KATHRYN. (*Frankly, decidedly.*) That appeals to me.

KATARINA (*More excited and embittered than before*) On the third day man said to his woman: "Go, woman, I don't want you any more. Go, you're free!"— And the woman went Then man said to himself: It's not good for man to be alone. So he created a woman after the image of his desire.

KATHRYN Happy the woman who fits the image of his desire. (KATARINA *turns her head sadly, to* HENRY, *embarrassedly.*) What else have you done, man in the stage of freedom? Tell us!

HENRY What else? I've bared the secrets of the creation. That I have done And I discovered that creation is nothing but . . nature, her miracles: formulas, her demons: formulas, her angles: formulas.

KATHRYN That can't be Everything alive lives from one breath, and that breath is holy. Do you know what that means: holy?

KATARINA. Right, my child!

HENRY. I only know that I understand nature! Yes
. . the old man must have created the world . . but
only I have understood it, and made her subject to my
will I have risen above mere earth and its childish laws

KATHRYN. What you're saying is marvelous

KATARINA Then the peasant slaughtered his oxen and
cow and said. "Begone! I don't need your dung to
fertilize my fields. For I need the fields no longer And I
don't need your milk to feed my children. For I need the
children no longer "

KATHRYN What you're saying is horrible

HENRY (*Emotionally*) "It is marvelous," "it is horrible!" Make your decision, girl Which is it?

KATHRYN It is marvelous and it is horrible

HENRY I offer you, image of my desire, a farm the
like of which the old man himself could not imagine in
his dreams I created it without him, but with his blessing

KATARINA. (*To* KATHRYN) Don't believe that!

HENRY Then with his sufferance.

KATARINA That is true (*Says this with effort only*)

HENRY (*To* KATHRYN, *triumphantly.*) There: She
admitted it!

KATARINA (*At once, with rising climax.*) On the
seventh day there comes from another part of the world
your neighbor and says "I see you've progressed far,
peasant Henry progressed far from God and from his
seed What you created is indeed a wondrous farm.
Only, without a harvest and without an earth It's a
wonderful farm. Only without a farmer Where are you,
peasant?" Thus asks your neighbor, and you remain
silent. You see, on your own farm you have starved to
death

HENRY (*Perturbed, he remains silent for a moment;
then, past* KATARINA, *he addresses* KATHRYN) Now
for everything in the world, tell us whom do you believe? Her, or me?

KATHRYN I can see the wonders you have created,
man, and I admire you for it. (HENRY *cries out jubi-*

lantly) But I also know that what the woman says is true (HENRY *attempts to reply*) You know it is true. And I pity you in your omnipotence, you poor, old man. But since in your world the woman can freely dispose of her life and body— (*To* KATARINA) and since I dread what you have prophesied, (*To* HENRY) —I will become your wife. (*She walks toward him and clings to him with a bodily gesture of surrender*)

HENRY. (*Holds her in his arms, shuddering with happiness*) Oh, Father in heaven, I thank you!

KATARINA (*Aside, without personal reaction*) So they bury you in the earth which was bequeathed to you by your father But the earth is without form and void, and the spirit of God moves above the waters.

CURTAIN

ACT FOUR

*The Center part of the stage is elevated, steps lead up to
it St Paul's Cathedral* HENRY *kneels, facing the
audience; somewhat in back of him,* KATHRYN *and*
KATE PARR.

HENRY Lord! Grant the people their pleas They arise
from the very depths of their times I don't know what
their needs of the moment happen to be—a plague, perhaps, or a revolution, or a war But I, at the very zenith
of my time, address you differently It's like this for
thirty-two years now I've been King of England, but at
the same time the centuries to come have passed by me,
much the same as have my beloved wives The age we
brought about—you tell me what went wrong! O Lord!
I flung a snowball—and behold an avalanche Lord!
(*As he raises his arms in a pious gesture, he discovers a
note stuck into the cuff of his sleeve Unfolds it, reads*)
"The Queen is exceedingly fond of the Chamberlain
Culpepper." Who might have slipped this to me? My
Archbishop (*Snickers*) The old buzzard! (*With a
tender, unsuspecting glance at* KATHRYN *he shifts from
one knee to the other, continues in previous voice*) Lord!
There are several things I'm not too happy about For
example. the war at the dawn of that late century Now,
this war to end wars could have been more noble, more
useful than any other But, what happened? It defeated
us all, victors and vanquished alike Then economics!
What went wrong with our cherished art of facts and
figures? It assumed the role of a force of nature and
haunts us with ebbs and flows as unpredictable as the
tides of a fifth element Yet you must admit that what
we've accomplished in our age is almost incredible
That's it! It's not credible any more! Lord! You per-
mitted mankind to travel the high road That was very
liberal of you, very enlightened But, just between us

51

doesn't some godly guile lurk behind it, eh? Not to say: a diabolical plot! (*Appeasingly.*) Joke, joke! (*Fervently*) Father in Heaven! Leave the world as we so magnificently completed it—leave it as it is. Leave well enough alone! (*Threateningly.*) I strongly advise it! (*Piously*) Amen. (*MUSIC.* HENRY *leads* KATHRYN *to rear, Left, where they bow, as if receiving blessing of Archbishop*)

KATE PARR. (*Has also risen, and at once comes to front, while LIGHTS change to broad daylight.*) Fresh air—fresh air! What an odd picture we must have presented—down on our knees! A self-centered monarch who chats with the God he pronounced dead like a speculator with a rich father-in-law. A frightened, devout queen who beseeches her Saviour for help, and a lady of the court who has studied too much to believe in anything (*ORGAN finishes,* KATE *exits.*)

(HENRY *and* KATHRYN *come to front, sit down on steps,* HENRY *stretches out and rests his head on* KATHRYN'S *lap.*)

HENRY. Ah! It's great to have a God with whom to share your sorrows and a young wife for your joys! I'm grateful that you made me young again.

KATHRYN It's my duty to bring you joy. I pray I'll never give you reason for sorrow.

HENRY. You never will. Unless it's because you're too good.

KATHRYN. I'm not good.

HENRY You are! Your antechamber is always crowded with petitioners and (*Tenderly*) you can never manage with your money.

KATHRYN. It's never enough, Henry There is so much misery It wouldn't be enough if I had a thousand times more

HENRY Charity adorns a monarch like a gem in his crown But within reason

KATHRYN Charity—within reason?

HENRY. As I said: you're too good

KATHRYN. (*Stubbornly.*) I'm not good. It's just that there is so much that troubles me.

HENRY. (*Shocked by her tone of voice*) No! Nothing must trouble you I'd rather pawn my crown Just tell the treasurer how much you need

KATHRYN (*Gratefully*) Thank you! If you only knew how great a favor you're granting me

HENRY It's only money Throw it away! But— (*Gently*) there's one small favor I ask in turn in your contacts with people be more sparing of your favors

KATHRYN My contacts with people? (HENRY *hands her the note, she reads it aloud, with a freezing voice*) "The Queen is exceedingly fond of the Chamberlain Culpepper "

HENRY (*Without changing his position*) Think nothing of it, my child, I know what it's worth A priest sent it Laugh it off! See, I'm laughing (*Begins to laugh, lightly at first, but when there is no echo, and* KATHRYN *stares rigidly ahead, his laughter grows more and more forced*) Why don't you laugh? I want you to laugh!

KATHRYN (*Strangely determined, compelled*) The Queen *is* exceedingly fond of the Chamberlain Culpepper!

HENRY That can't be!

KATHRYN It is!

HENRY Say no more!

KATHRYN (*Compelled*) I must tell you!

HENRY Tell me what?

KATHRYN Everything

HENRY Everything? (*Ducks under the word*) Never —never tell me everything! (*Now the typical escape maneuver*) Ah, now I understand! The Widow Parr and her libertine nonsense! The Parr, the Parr, the Parr! It's all her fault!

KATHRYN Kate has nothing to do with it!

HENRY It must be the Parr's fault! It is the Parr's fault!

KATHRYN. No!

HENRY The Parr must leave the court at once

KATHRYN Leave? The only human being I found in this snake-pit?

HENRY (*Struck by her words*) Snake-pit? The only human . ? (*Stares at her, deeply shocked*) Widow Parr!

(KATE *enters from Right.*)

KATHRYN Oh, Kate! (*Falls into her arms with a sob*)

HENRY. (*With his back turned*) Widow Parr! It pleases the Queen to dispense with your services

KATHRYN. She's only honest, and good.

KATE (*Still embracing* KATHRYN) It doesn't surprise me that His Majesty dismisses me —But I am surprised that Your Majesty lacks the courage to look me in the eye (HENRY *forces himself to look at her Tastes effect*) God save the Queen! (*Kisses* KATHRYN *on forehead, walks slowly to rear, Left* KATHRYN *breaks into tears.*)

HENRY. (*Clings to her*) God save the Queen!

(*LIGHTS on rear, Left,* KATARINA OF ARGON *enters*)

'KATE O, Katarina! How can we save the Queen?

KATARINA I don't know, Kate (*Puts arm around her, leads her to front, where both crouch down*)

KATE It is always the same lie. Whether he banishes you for the sake of his conscience, or sends another to the block for the sake of morals . .

KATARINA. . . whether he, the modern man, massacres heathens for the sake of their salvation, or wages war in the name of peace, and subjugates peoples in the name of freedom, whether he finally contaminates nature everywhere and destroys mankind for the sake of civilization . . .

KATE . it is always the same lie .

HENRY. Say what you wish, women, poets, priests and prophets! This is the road upon which mankind has embarked. You'll never succeed in diverting man from his course, nor in turning the steel of his machinery back into the ore from whence it came!

KATHRYN. That's not their intention.

HENRY. Then what is?

KATHRYN. (*Spontaneous outburst*) Oh, Henry! Can't you see how man fares in your world? He suffers and you feel nothing. He looks to you, and you don't recognize him. He speaks to you, and you don't hear him You let him slip quietly from your side, and perish—like the swan in the reeds when winter comes.

HENRY. (*Looks at her.*) Yes,—it's true. Great is the cold But there's no recourse— The consequence of thought is. more thinking. The consequence of invention is more inventing The consequence of power is more power. There is no other way

KATARINA Is there no other way? The ways of the world have never been that cut and dried! Could they become that simple towards the end? I wonder

KATE I can see man become a victim of the laws which he himself set into motion

HENRY. I know what troubles you. You fear the uncertainty of the high noon

KATHRYN I fear the night.

HENRY No night will fall, my child Believe me

KATHRYN (*Desperately*) I believe you

KATE. One slight hope remains. fear.

KATARINA Fear—a hope?

KATE The universal fear of universal destruction.

(KATE *and* KATARINA *exit to Left, LIGHTS back on* HENRY *and* KATHRYN)

HENRY. You're trembling, dearest

KATHRYN. Hold me close

HENRY Are you cold?

KATHRYN I don't want to end like Anne Boleyn I'll tell you everything if you promise me mercy.

HENRY. Hush! Hush! I'll grant you mercy if you tell

me nothing Hush! Don't move. Don't spoil the peace of this beautiful evening I can see a tiny cloud above— white and curved like your body. It's all alone—a lonely swimmer in a vast, vast ocean

KATHRYN (*Abrupt, clear voice*) My education at Norfolk Castle was very thorough We had a music teacher, a melancholy young man named Mannox One day, during a voice lesson, he kissed me I pushed him away and he fell into the harp Afterwards I felt sorry for what I'd done—and I admitted him into my chamber He taught me much I didn't know It frightened me at first, but I soon got used to it

HENRY (*From afar*) How old were you?

KATHRYN Thirteen (*Awaits his reaction, when none comes forth, she goes on*) Soon my cousins found out about it, and they wanted their share There were a lot of young men at the castle, chamberlains and pages, among them Culpepper While our aunt was asleep we took our pleasure with each other.

HENRY That must have been much fun

KATHRYN It was We invented gallant games For example. the Henriade We re-enacted the marriage comedies of our King

HENRY (*First sign of reaction*) The marriage comedies of your King? You re-enacted that? Without a stage?

KATHRYN. We only needed a bed Usually I was Anne Boleyn.

HENRY Yes, that is your role. And who was—your partner?

KATHRYN. They took turns.

HENRY You were very liberal

KATHRYN We followed your teachings

HENRY Whose teachings?

KATHRYN The teachings of the freed spirit of the modern age You preached that the girl, too, is a human being and free to dispose of her body We readily understood that (*Livelier*) But I only accepted gentlemen of rank—except for the first one, Mannox.

HENRY. The melancholy musician.

KATHRYN. Yes. He became envious when we excluded him, so he told my aunt. She thought it best to send me away from Norfolk Castle. That's how I came to stay with Katarina

HENRY. (*Weakly*) Why have you told me all this?

KATHRYN. Now that you know I can't be blackmailed any more. The playmates of my youth have placed a high price on their silence. But now you know everything. Now I can breathe again (HENRY *shaken by sobs. Clings to him, touched.*) Please, don't, darling, don't be sad. Rejoice that you have a loyal, honest wife. Nothing has happened beyond what I confessed.

HENRY. (*Tonelessly*) Nothing has happened?

KATHRYN. (*Unaffected.*) No

HENRY. (*Lamenting*) Why did you tell me?

KATHRYN. Because I realized that you knew about it

HENRY. (*Yelling*) What did I know? That the Queen is exceedingly fond of the Chamberlain Culpepper! So— so what! So you blabber out everything, you sweet innocent, you!

KATHRYN. Whether you knew it or not. I'm glad I confessed everything

HENRY Ah, if people confessed everything that plagues their conscience, they would have exterminated each other long ago—and I'd be the only man left in the world Only because of the lie, and because no one can look into another person's heart, does mankind still exist

KATHRYN You were bound to find out about it

HENRY If anyone had dared to say evil about you I would have had him beheaded! Now I must have you beheaded.

KATHRYN No!

HENRY. (*Sadly.*) Yes, my child.

KATHRYN. You can't do that!

HENRY. No—but I must!

KATHRYN. I've confessed to have your forgiveness (*On her knees, in front of him*) Forgive me, Henry, and everything will be all right! Think of how happy we've been with each other until this moment. I made you young again in those two years.

HENRY In two minutes you've made me old.

KATHRYN. I'll make it up to you. Just look at me, and you'll know it

HENRY How could you accept my proposal?

KATHRYN. I didn't want to.

HENRY But you did accept it! Why?

KATHRYN Obedience and—pity.

HENRY. Pity?

KATHRYN Now have pity on me!

HENRY You married me—out of pity?

KATHRYN What else did you think? Out of love?

HENRY (*Stunned*) I'm Henry Tudor, beloved by my people, envied by my contemporaries for the magnificence of my life! My spirit is immortal Why would anyone pity me?

KATHRYN. Because of the misfortune Katarina predicted will overtake your spirit . . .

HENRY .   misfortune?

KATHRYN It swayed me, and I told you that, too One must merely look at you, the way you toss your weight around   like a beetle on its back It's enough to make any girl feel pity

HENRY You were dressed like a nun. But lewdness marked your body Why did you keep it a secret?

KATHRYN. You approved of it.

HENRY I approved?

KATHRYN You said that the woman, too, was free to dispose of her body .   .

HENRY It wasn't meant that way.

KATHRYN I can see that now It's always meant just the way you mean it now, the way it suits you. When you desire a woman she should be free to dispose of her body When you have her, she should never have done so before

HENRY (*Stunned momentarily*) I stand before you not as a husband, nor as a philosopher, but as the supreme judge of the realm As a husband I'd forgive you, as a philosopher I'd acquit you As a judge I must condemn you because you disgraced the King's bed

KATHRYN Disgraced your bed? I didn't know anyone could disgrace your bed' Then you might as well know how repulsive you are with your clumsy, sweaty attempts—usually in vain' And what you then demand of me is revolting' I'm glad I've finally told you how I really feel'

HENRY (*Steps back, ducks under her invective, then catches himself surprisingly*) Hush, hush, hush—don't remind me of those blissful hours You were so full of love, so lascivious, so knowing, too, I often wondered I need you alive' (*Kneels before her*) Kathryn, Kathryn, I beg you to remain with me I implore you to tell me how I can spare your life'

KATHRYN (*Strange and cold*) You know that is impossible I've lied enough in my days I don't want to lie any more I can't It is choking me (*Her hand indicates her neck*)

HENRY (*Sinister*) Where?

(KATHRYN *still clutching her neck, understands, and collapses*)

(*LIGHTS off*)

CURTAIN

ACT FIVE

LIGHTS on Raised platform, as in previous scene. Room in Westminster Above the steps a heavy, deep armchair.

KATE (*Enters.*) One day the King appears before parliament and announces that he—after the sad experience with his fifth wife—is grimly determined never to marry again Should he, however, permit himself to be swayed for the good of his people and take yet another wife, then anyone who suppresses information that the bride is unchaste, shall be guilty of treason. Four short weeks later the bells in London ring The King does marry. He marries, to be absolutely certain there'll be no disappointment, a widow (*Laughs*) He marries—me! (HENRY *enters from Right, with a gout-ridden walk.*) Oh, yes! The famous innovator has grown old. The perpetual bridegroom now desires a wife—to nurse his ailments That I've done since our wedding—and with remarkable success (*She embraces and kisses him.* HENRY *purrs,* KATE *continues, to audience*) Only when he keeps bragging about the accomplishments in this late century—and I can't hold back my own ideas, does he throw a fit . .

HENRY (*Not on cue*) Oh, Kate!—You're such a good wife Too bad you're such a professor.

KATE I just can't conceal from him what I think . . .

HENRY. (*Furrows brow.*)

KATE (*As if handing him medicine*) Your medicine.

HENRY. (*As if taking it, then, trying to provoke her.*) Yes, medicine What a boon to mankind it became in this late century — (*Threateningly*) Eh?

KATE (*Sincere.*) Remarkable

HENRY Take the French disease! What a plague it was to our men and women! A sword above our beds.

60

A thorn in the flesh. And today? Vanished. Extinguished
by research. Once again, lovers can take tender pleasure
of each other—without suspicion and fear—as in Ho-
mer's time.

KATE And in exchange we have other ailments that
are far more murderous and of a less—gallant origin.

HENRY What?

KATE. I was just saying.

.HENRY. Damn—damn—damn! Am I never to start
my day without wanting to jump out of my skin? Am
I never to say one word without an echo telling me it
knows better? (*Runs up and down, blusteringly*) Man
creates a world with wit and finesse—and on the seventh
day comes the woman and proves that it's good-for-
nothing, just vain bungling. (*Hisses at her.*) Vain bungling, eh? And why? Because you women lack brains.
You're just flesh that attaches itself to our intellect—
deadly, but decidedly blissful. But this I prophesy:
you'll teach your tongue to stop contradicting me or our
wedded bliss'll end most abruptly and horribly: either
I'll suffer a heart attack or—I'll suddenly survive you!
(*Stiffens with a sudden cry of pain*) Kate! Kate!

KATE. Oh, dear! What's the matter? Is it your heart?
(HENRY, *with clenched lips, points to leg.*) The leg!
What a relief! (*Helps him to chair.*) Better ten times the
leg than once the heart! (*Rolls up his trouserleg.*) The
air already refreshes the throbbing flesh. And now I'll
cool the sores (*Treats leg.*) Ah, that's better, that's
better Life is already becoming beautiful again (HENRY
grimly shakes head in denial) It's all right! The gout,
that's an honest, old male disease. Always remember
that After all, you know what caused it Think of the
great, great herd of pigs you've eaten in your lifetime,
and how you enjoyed every single bite.

HENRY. (*Emotional*) Oh, Kate: you're such a good
woman Kiss me.

KATE Easy, easy! (*Kisses him.*)

HENRY You're such a good wife.

KATE (*With a sigh.*) Yes, I am

HENRY Too bad you're an old professor and against progress

KATE (*Refers to leg*) Is it getting better?

HENRY (*Morosely*) No! But we did make progress! Incredible progress! Around 1500 man's lifespan was thirty-one years Now fifty-nine

KATE (*Gestures with hand*) Ah!

HENRY My dear wife these are exact figures

KATE I don't believe in figures

HENRY What?

KATE Figures don't tell the truth

HENRY. You don't believe that two times two makes four?

KATE. Possibly. But . . .

HENRY This I'm anxious to hear

KATE. For example. you'll go down in history as the King who had six wives That's the figure The truth is that you had no wife (HENRY *howls* KATE *appeasingly*) I was just saying

HENRY (*Blissfully*) Quiet! (*About leg*) There! It's going away. Aahh! Bliss, bliss spreads through the poor flesh.

KATE. Didn't I promise you? Now you can straighten up again.

HENRY Embrace me, Kate Love me!

KATE. (*In his arms, with honest impulse*) Oh, just what is it that makes everyone love you—you monster!

HENRY Because I'm strong and pure The people sense it, women sense it They revere in me the spirit of humanism that at long last is bringing a lasting peace to the world

KATE Oh, please no! Let us not talk politics

HENRY I'm talking about peace.

KATE When I hear peace, I see war

HENRY I've won two world wars they were the last!

KATE You make that sound as if you're saying you've survived a couple of strokes Now mankind lies prostrate while awaiting a third and probably fatal one . . .

HENRY. Don't worry, my dear, there won't be another.

KATE. Are you sure?

HENRY. Absolutely.

KATE. But lately there was a close call: when they fought for a tip of Asia, and a famous general wanted to employ the ultimate weapon.

HENRY. Yes, but the president recalled him to maintain the peace of the world.

KATE. Then the life of mankind actually depended on one man.

HENRY. (*Gently superior.*) Wrong, Professor. Let me teach you something Neither kings nor presidents decide any more whether there'll be war or peace . . .

KATE. Then who does?

HENRY. The calculating machine, the electronic brain. It happened, Kate: the president employed these marvelous mechanisms to compute how the world of facts and figures would react.

KATE (*Beside herself*) But that's horrible! Then mankind owes the peace not even to a man, but to machines

HENRY. We don't want to talk politics.

KATE. I'm talking about man! (*Belligerently.*) If mankind, split as it is by ideologies into two armed camps, is governed by the belief in the supremacy of reason, then where, in all this enlightenment, remains . . . man?

HENRY. That's what the struggle is about. Look what is happening to man in the East . . .

KATE. Whether I look to the East or to the West, it is the spirit of the modern age that I perceive. Both are branches from the same tree.

HENRY. But in the East man is just a number . . .

KATE. True. But how do you prevent man from becoming just that? With the calculating machine? Encounter the freezing over of life as it threatens from the East, with what? The freezing over of the West? I'm just a foolish woman, but this I know: the future belongs to those from both worlds who can overcome the spirit out of which both developed: the belief that to calculate is bliss!

HENRY Why do you tell me that?

KATE. The calculating machine as the conscience of mankind . . . that is your doing . . .

HENRY. (*Sinister*) What? How?

KATE. Because you used your conscience as a calculating machine (HENRY *stiffens momentarily, then advances threateningly.*) With Your Majesty's permission I'm expecting a visitor

HENRY. (*Takes deep breath*) It's all right I need time I'm preoccupied with ideas that far overshadow what bothers you, and I don't know how much more time my God has measured out for me Come here, Kate (*Takes her into arms, kisses her.*) Don't try to change me, but you, too, remain as you are.

(ANNA OF CLEVES *appears, front Right*)

HENRY. Now go and entertain your visitor. Do I know him?

KATE Yes. (*Maliciously.*) Fleetingly. (HENRY *releases her with a slap on her behind Then, with a clinging gaze, he watches her leave, and exits. Heartily*) Anna of Cleves! (ANNA *curtsies,* KATE *takes her by the hand.*) I'm happy to meet my husband's former wife (*Offers* ANNA *a chair, she sits down mechanically, stares at* KATE *speechlessly.*) I'm grateful, Anna, that the great distance hasn't discouraged you from visiting me Why aren't you talking?

ANNA. Ma'am, if I'm speechless it's because I imagined you to be—entirely different.

KATE The King has not yet ordered coins minted with my image.

ANNA It doesn't pay, not according to experience Oh, forgive me I'm very straightforward

KATE. I prefer it.

ANNA. How's he getting on?

KATE. He suffers from the gout And then his heart—

ANNA Don't you worry! He'll outlive a few more
wives (KATE *laughs amusedly*) Oh, forgive me But
that's why I came I came to warn you

KATE Warn me?

ANNA You're doomed unless you escape at once!

KATE What?

ANNA I've written to my brother, the Duke of Cleves
He's looking forward to meeting you, my brother is, with
real pleasure A very impressive man, my brother,
austere, a lover of music, and still available

KATE But why? What do I have to fear?

ANNA You don't seem to understand All right then!
You know that I live almost at the end of the world But
a mere two hours from my forest is Norfolk Castle.
Kathryn, it's common gossip, even among my swine-
herds, how you used to carry on while under the care of
your good aunt (KATE *attempts to say something*) Oh,
please don't misunderstand! I think what you did was
priceless Really! I envy you your sunny youth But if
the King should find out . . ! Save your head! Escape
to Cleves I've figured everything   .

KATE (*Smilingly*) Figured! Everything! Just like
Henry! You mean well, Anna But you're wrong You've
left out the one figure which he, too, often overlooks
Your mistake is one human being The Katherine you
came to warn is Kathryn Howard, and she has already
put her head on the block

ANNA (*Deeply astonished*) No!

KATE That "no" is also his You're truly the King's
sister.

ANNA Then, Ma'am, you are the next Katherine? Just
think of it But didn't I sense it right away My nose

KATE Thank you, Anna, for your good intentions and
for your courage It's necessary indeed that we women
stick together

ANNA Then I can be of service to you after all?
Have you a past?

KATE O, yes.

ANNA Ahhh!

KATE I was twice widowed when he married me.

ANNA Au! That's a good one! Wonderful! Congratulations!—You know, I've also plowed two under, two sturdy knights, may they rest in peace No, no one can cope with me—except him. He's so strong, so wise, so good, (*Dreamily*) so brutal!

HENRY (*Offstage*) Kate! Kate!

KATE (*Alarmed*) O, my God! (*Hurries to Left, while* ANNA *exits as LIGHTS change*)

HENRY (*Enters, as if walking in a dream.*) Kate! Kate!

KATE Henry! Is it the leg?

HENRY This time it's the heart!

KATE (*Soothingly*) No! (*Leads him to chair.*)

HENRY You shouldn't always contradict me (*Seated.*) Yes! Who would have thought that I, too, should have to die! (*Laughs softly*) Ha! The way I know myself, I ought to be struggling against it I've no time to die I'm indispensable! But instead, like any other human being, I crawl away, and turn into decay It doesn't really matter, I can see that now Kate, why aren't you contradicting me?

KATE (*Swallows*) I can see that, too

HENRY At last! Now, at long last! It makes me happy, Kate Now, please go fetch . . .

KATE The doctor!

HENRY No! What for?! The Archbishop. No! No priest Call my wife! Forgive me, dearest, I mean—

KATE (*Pleasantly*) It's all right She'll be here

HENRY Thank you (*Excitedly*) But now, so that it continues after I'm gone, so that they know what to do— please, write! Write what I dictate! Write! (KATE *crouches down, pretends to, but does not write Dictates unsteadily, with fluttering gestures, but presents themes clearly*) Hold fast to the new faith! Knowledge is power! What you discover, subdue! The universe is discovered! Paragraph Earth of no further interest Only as a base Global discord therefore ridiculous Achieve unity on basis of ideals common to both sides

economy as the philosophy of life, statistics as ethics!
Peace on earth' Paragraph Raise your eyes to the stars,
and colonize them! Theological question Does original
sin apply to the inhabitants of other planets? If so—
hold missionaries and firewood in readiness! Much remains to be done! Plan ahead. First aim only at objects
suitable for settlement and exploitation! Then regulate
the movement of the planets! Later bring order into the
Milky Way! Later standardize the remaining nebulae
Paragraph What else is there? Oh, yes don't forget
God! (*He rises,* KATE *attempts to prevent it*) Don't
forget God! (*He rushes back and forth with strictly
defined movements*) Brothers, somewhere above the
firmament lives a dear Father! Search for God· top
priority project! Crash program to find God! When God
is found— (*To himself*) yes, what then? (*Blusteringly*)
Better make damn sure you treat him decently Be
friendly, be tactful, be—Christian toward Him! (*He
now stands on platform*) Remember Holy is the Lord,
and it was His will that man's intellect—shall compre-
hend and redeem—God's dumb world! Kate, I'm dizzy!
(*In order to balance himself he spreads his arms, and
now stands in the same position as he had stood in Act
One, only now he wavers*) Kate, where are you? I can't
see you any more

(KATE *stares at* KATARINA, *who has entered from Left*)

KATARINA (*Also in same spot as in Act One, quietly*)
Can you see me, Henry Tudor?
HENRY (*Arms still spread, tamely*) Yes, Katarina, I
can see you, you, my wife, my good conscience
KATARINA I was that until the hour when you stood
as you're standing now, and began to talk like this
KATE. He's delirious.
KATARINA No He has merely concluded a thought
he then began (*Both* WOMEN *lead* HENRY *to chair,
Center, make him comfortable.*)

HENRY   (*Senile.*) What we undertook—was something new

KATARINA. It was something that otherwise might never have occurred to mankind.

HENRY   We subdued the earth according to God's command

KATARINA   You subdued it—but not according to God's command   You look at creation as nature· therein lie all the sense and nonsense of your age.

HENRY. Nonsense?

KATARINA   Look at the result. Look at the condition man is in

HENRY   What condition is he in?

KATARINA   The same as you —superior to the highest, and wallowing in the depths   By denying the creator you betrayed the creature   By doing away with God, you did away with man

HENRY   (*Lazily*)   Entirely possible mankind will be destroyed

KATARINA   With all its magnificent achievements it will be destroyed tomorrow unless something happens today

KATE   Perhaps it has happened! A great physicist has said that the universe is not a huge machine, but a bold conception

HENRY   (*Momentarily surprised, then*)   Theories! Tomorrow there'll be others

KATARINA   (*After a pause*)   No, Henry! Science's latest equation equals the oldest prayer: "Our father, which art in heaven" The end of your progression away from God, the final discovery—is the discovery of God. And this, Henry Tudor, is the end of modern age.

HENRY   (*Slyly*)   Now you see, Katarina, that makes sense: that modern age comes to an end when I leave the earth. But the reason I asked for you, Katarina (KATE *moves away.*) before I leave it seems only proper that I should make confession.

KATARINA. Yes.

HENRY. Yes . . . but confess what?

KATARINA Just once refuse to listen to that voice you call your conscience, but be honest

HENRY I'll be completely honest, so that God will grant me even more eternal salvation

KATARINA Henry! Deals up to the last minute?

HENRY (*Bravely*) Tell me what I shall do!

KATARINA Look above you! Become aware again of the creator!

HENRY But what shall I tell my flock?

KATARINA The same!

HENRY They won't recognize the creator, they know too much (*After a short deliberation*) No, my dearest. You will have to tell them. (*Smiling*) One can become the herald of a new age just once. What to make of my heritage is now up to you, but leave me my peace— My good wives! Who will care for you when I'm no longer among you! Who, in these difficult times, will espouse the cause of mankind! Oh—we are to be pitied for my passing!

(*LIGHTS off* HENRY KATARINA *remains standing*, KATE *is kneeling, as are the other* WIVES *who have entered from both sides*)

KATARINA. Here rests a man born of the weakness of the flesh lived for the supremacy of reason died overpowered by his own power. You, who pass by, pray for the peace of his soul pray—and go on— And now, sisters, rise and cry no longer.

ANNA OF CLEVES (*Hastily.*) Right. We had reason enough to cry while he was alive Let our memory of him be happy, and let us share his heritage.

KATARINA. Yes, we must accept it: they are the values of his age. Kate, please!

KATE. He left it in six shares.

ANNA OF CLEVES (*Hungrily.*) What is the first?

KATE. His conscience. (ANNA OF CLEVES *retreats, frightened.* OTHERS *do not move.*) It is the conscience that he guided his flock with.

KATARINA (*Smilingly*) Was he the shepherd?

JANE SEYMOUR (*Heavily*) Not the shepherd, but the sheep dog who drove it from the Lord's pastures But, I will take his conscience.

KATE. Then his gold

ANNA OF CLEVES (*Quickly*) Oh, I'll be glad to take it off your hands

KATE (*Smiles Then*) Then· his love.

KATHRYN I should like to have it

ANNE BOLEYN (*Carefully*) Do you know what you're asking, my child? Don't you think I'm entitled to it?

KATHRYN. Oh, Anne Boleyn! What wouldn't he do for you! And what did he ever do for me? Nothing but fill me with fear and disgust.

ANNE BOLEYN Didn't you love him?

KATHRYN. That lecherous old man?

ANNE BOLEYN. He was a young and handsome and strong man. I love him.

KATHRYN. (*After a pause*) Then it is yours. (ANNE BOLEYN *accepts* KATHRYN'S *gesture gratefully*.)

KATE. His freedom.

KATHRYN. (*Bitter.*) Yes, his freedom, that is my share!

KATE Then—the new wisdom.

KATARINA. You're entitled to it.

KATE. Because it held me enthralled?

KATARINA. Yes—but you rose above it.

KATE. Finally: his spirit.

KATARINA. It was not his spirit He merely made it his own. (*Slowly LIGHTS off all* WOMEN *except* KATARINA.) It is the spirit that, in eternal dissatisfaction, forever cries out for more experience, but seeks only: gold, state and power. It was the forceful, restless surge of a mighty age. But that age is now near its end. A new one approaches. It must be different, or there'll never be another for the creatures of this earth. (*LIGHTS off* KATARINA.)

FINAL CURTAIN

OTHER TITLES AVAILABLE FROM SAMUEL FRENCH

OUTRAGE
Itamar Moses

Drama / 8m, 2f / Unit Set

In Ancient Greece, Socrates is accused of corrupting the young with his practice of questioning commonly held beliefs. In Renaissance Italy, a simple miller named Menocchio runs afoul of the Inquisition when he develops his own theory of the cosmos. In Nazi Germany, the playwright Bertolt Brecht is persecuted for work that challenges authority. And in present day New England, a graduate student finds himself in the center of a power struggle over the future of the University. An irreverent epic that spans thousands of years, *Outrage* explores the power of martyrdom, the power of theatre, and how the revolutionary of one era become the tyrant of the next.

www.ingramcontent.com/pod-product-compliance
Lightning Source LLC
Chambersburg PA
CBHW070648120726
47909CB00004B/1636